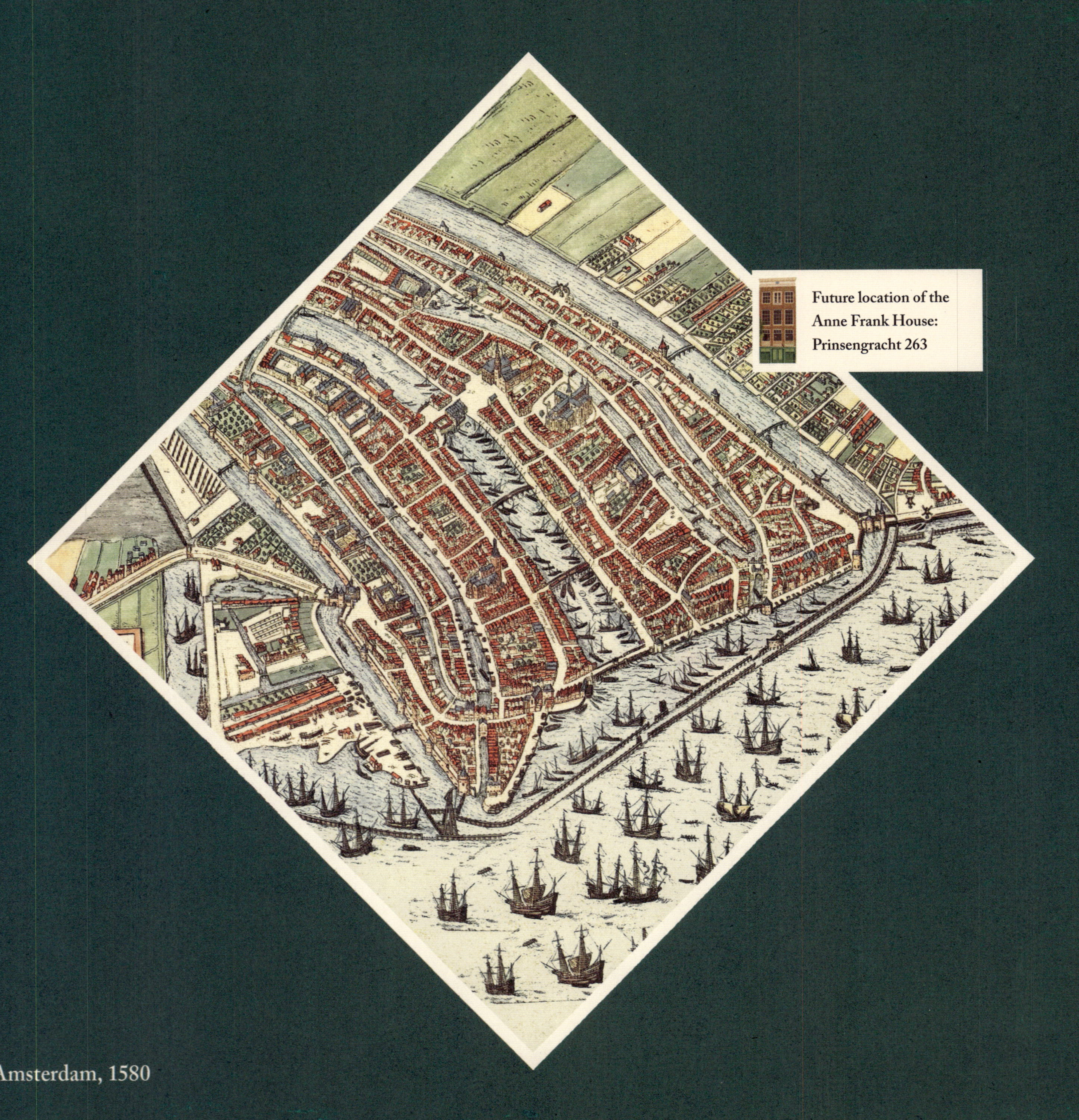

Amsterdam, 1580

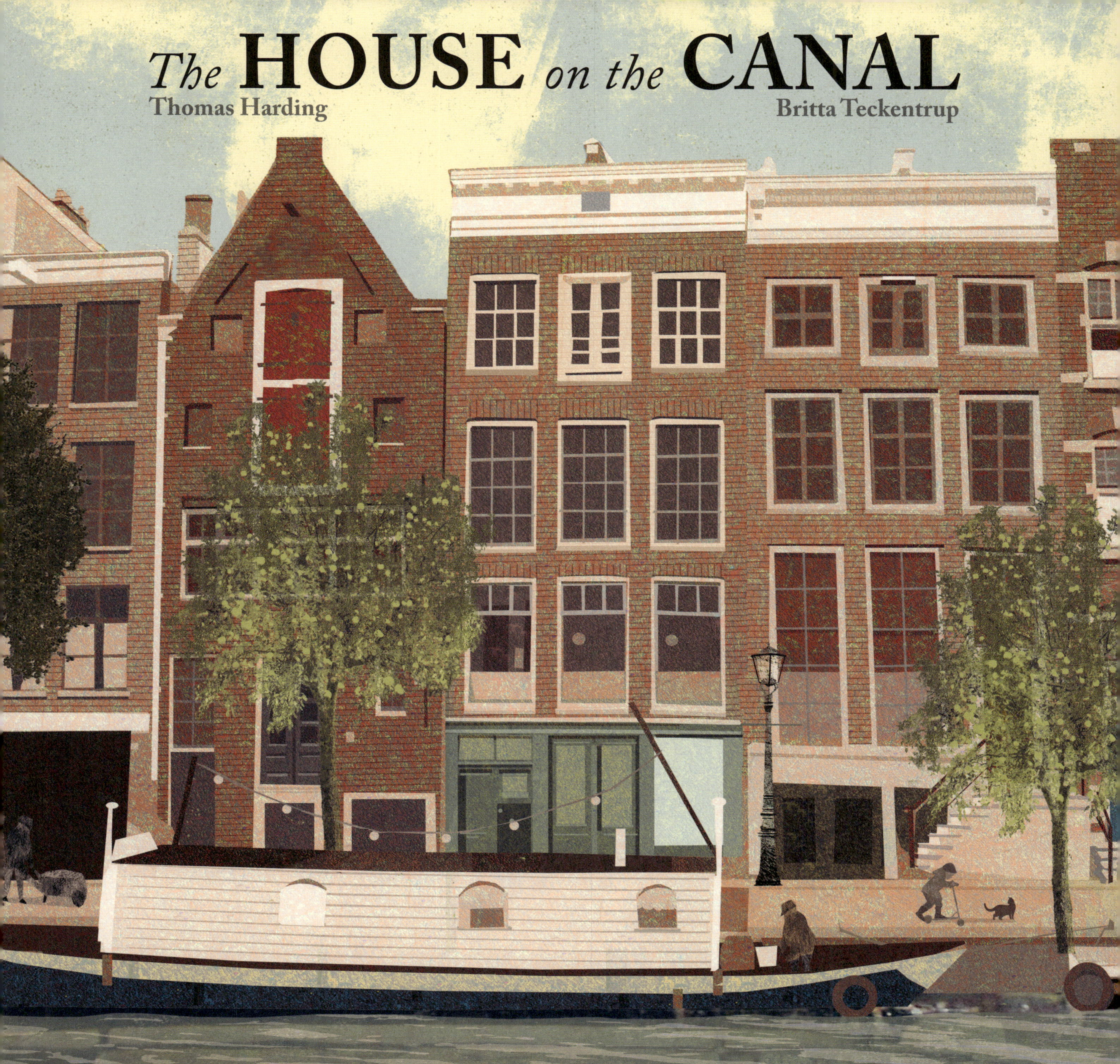
The HOUSE on the CANAL
Thomas Harding
Britta Teckentrup

The "Back House", 1954

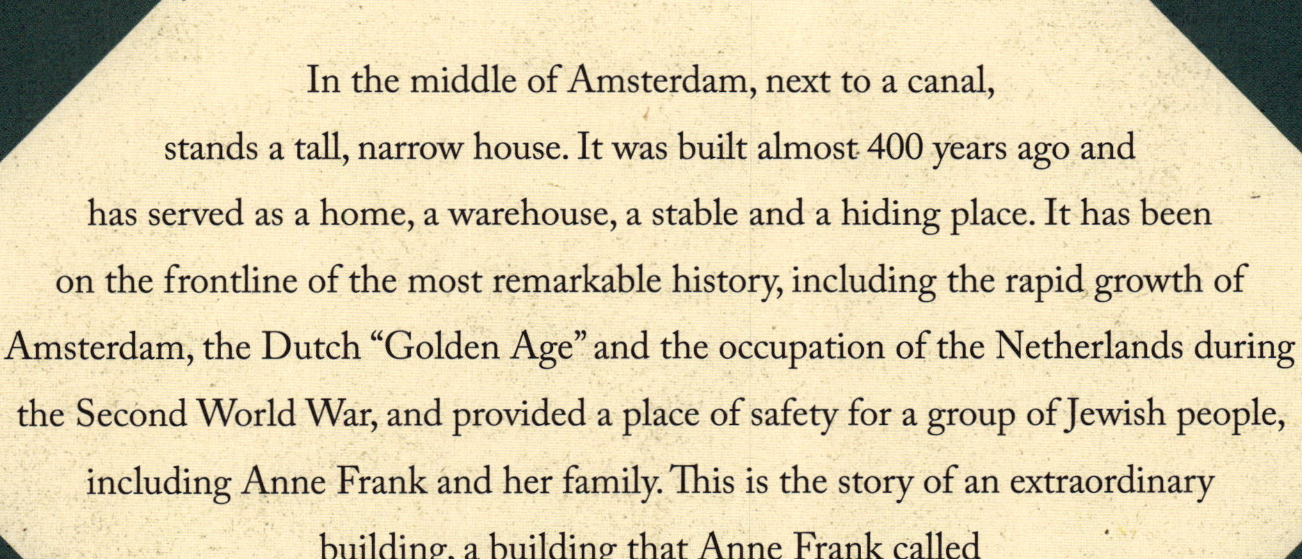

In the middle of Amsterdam, next to a canal, stands a tall, narrow house. It was built almost 400 years ago and has served as a home, a warehouse, a stable and a hiding place. It has been on the frontline of the most remarkable history, including the rapid growth of Amsterdam, the Dutch "Golden Age" and the occupation of the Netherlands during the Second World War, and provided a place of safety for a group of Jewish people, including Anne Frank and her family. This is the story of an extraordinary building, a building that Anne Frank called "the old house on the canal".

A long time ago, there was a little piece of marshland. With some cows. A few herons.
A family of fieldmice. And in the sky above, a flock of seagulls.
It was a calm and happy place.

The sun rose. The cows chewed the grass. The herons searched for tasty fish. The fieldmice scurried and sniffed and scurried some more. The seagulls swooped and squawked. And then the sun went down. Years passed, but little changed.

Then there was a new sound. The bump and babble of humans as the city grew closer and closer. There were so many people. They had come from places far away, hoping for calm, quiet, happy lives. One day, men and women arrived, carrying shovels and pushing carts.

They dug a long ditch through the damp, muddy earth. With wood and bricks they built strong walls along each bank. They let water in to make a canal. Next they spread the dirt over the land, building it high above the water, and covered it with fine sand from the beach.

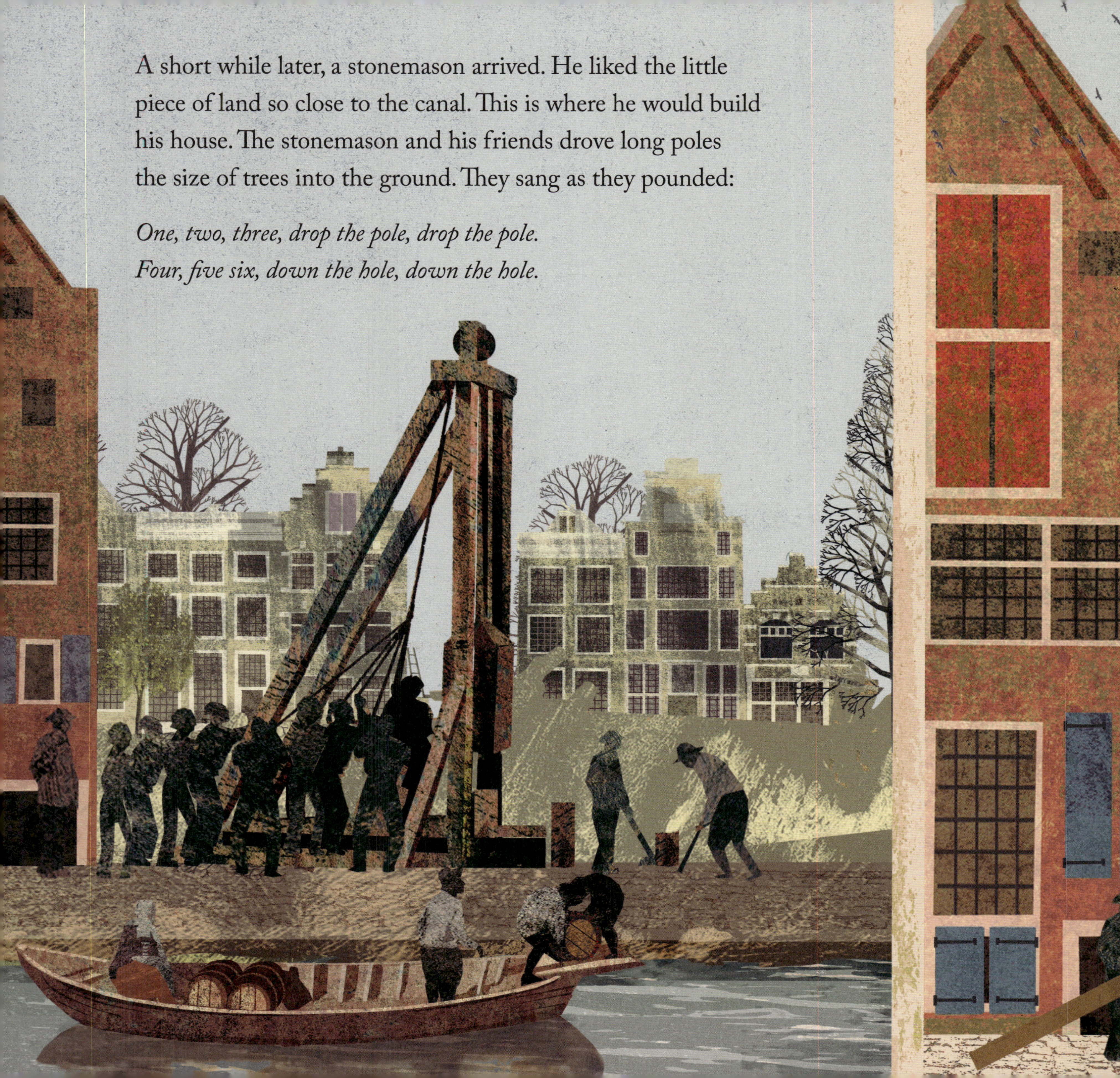

A short while later, a stonemason arrived. He liked the little piece of land so close to the canal. This is where he would build his house. The stonemason and his friends drove long poles the size of trees into the ground. They sang as they pounded:

One, two, three, drop the pole, drop the pole.
Four, five six, down the hole, down the hole.

They built a lovely house with strong brick walls, sturdy pine floors and a green front door. The stonemason wanted more space. So they added an annexe behind the main house with a large attic. Once the house on the canal was finished, they celebrated with a party.

Houses were built on either side. One with a pointy roof, another with a roof flat. One with blue shutters, another with shutters red.

A tall church was built nearby. Its bells rang –
DONG DONG DONG DONG –
four times every hour.

A young woman moved into the house on the canal with her twelve children. They had been chased away from their old home because of their Christian beliefs. They loved the new place with its strong brick walls, sturdy pine floors and green front door. It made them feel safe. In spring, the young children planted flowers in the large garden behind the house. In summer, they picked fruit from the trees.

In the winter, they skated on the frozen canal and drank warm milk by the fire. This was a happy house.

1663

1709

But then the plague arrived and sickness spread along the canal. The young woman and her family could not go outside. They could not see their friends. They waited and waited and waited. It seemed like for ever.

Until one day it was over, and they could go outside again.

Many years passed. The young woman grew old, and her children moved away. Rain came through the roof, the floors rotted and the windows cracked.

Winter brought a Great Frost. It was so cold the canal froze for weeks and weeks. Boats could not bring food and water to the people who lived near the canal.

A wealthy merchant and his wife moved into the house on the canal. The windows were painted and the floors were fixed. The annexe was replaced and the pointy roof was changed to a flat one. They had no children, but there was a maid and a cook and many fine friends who came to visit their lovely house.

Soon there was dancing and fun at the house, and candles flickered merrily in the shiny windows.

Thirty summers passed by and the wealthy merchant and his wife grew old. One morning, the old merchant did not wake up, and his wife moved away. The windows cracked, and the paint peeled on the green front door. Darkness drew across the house like a thick curtain.

Winters came and went and came and went again. The house shivered, empty and cold. Then five large horses came to stay. They slept on straw spread out on the ground floor. It was warm and dry. At night, they were kept company by spiders and mice and bats. And the church bells rang – *DONG DONG DONG DONG* – four times every hour.

1841

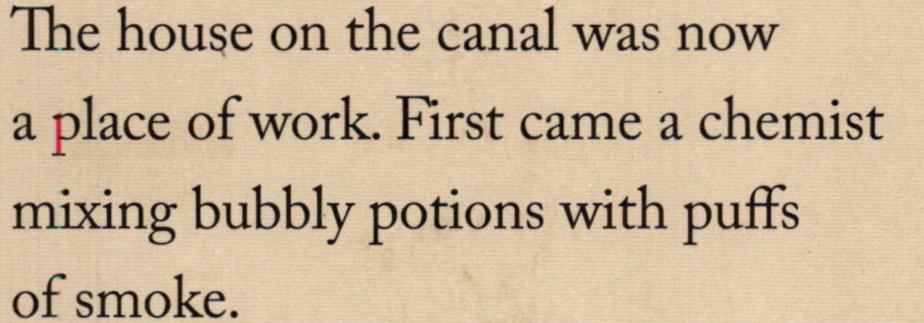

The house on the canal was now a place of work. First came a chemist mixing bubbly potions with puffs of smoke.

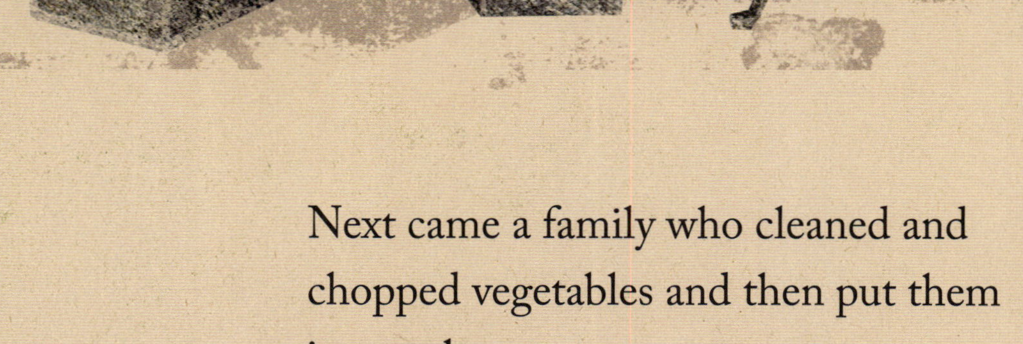

Next came a family who cleaned and chopped vegetables and then put them in metal cans.

1853

Once more, the house was full of sounds and smells and industry.

And in the garden behind the house, a little chestnut tree took root.

More and more people lived at the house.
They lived next to the canal in the front.
And they lived in the annexe at the back of the house.
They burned peat in the fireplaces and flushed
their toilets into the canal. A blue haze hung
along the street.

The air smelled of rotten eggs.

1880

Late one night, the bells in the clock tower had just rung thrice when the call came: *Fire! Fire!* Burning flames burst from the chimney, boiling and battering and blistering the strong brick walls and sturdy pine floors and green front door.

Four horses galloped up the canal pulling a water wagon. The brave firefighters saved the house.

1884

An ironmonger, his wife and children arrived at the house. From a burning hot fire he made metal beds and iron stoves. The children loved the house, bringing laughter and light into its dark and dusty corners. They played with the rabbits in the garden and fed the chickens. And in the garden, the chestnut tree grew and grew.

As the moon rose,
and with bravery in their hearts,
the children crawled along the roof
between the front house and the annexe.

The house was once again filled with
songs and joy.

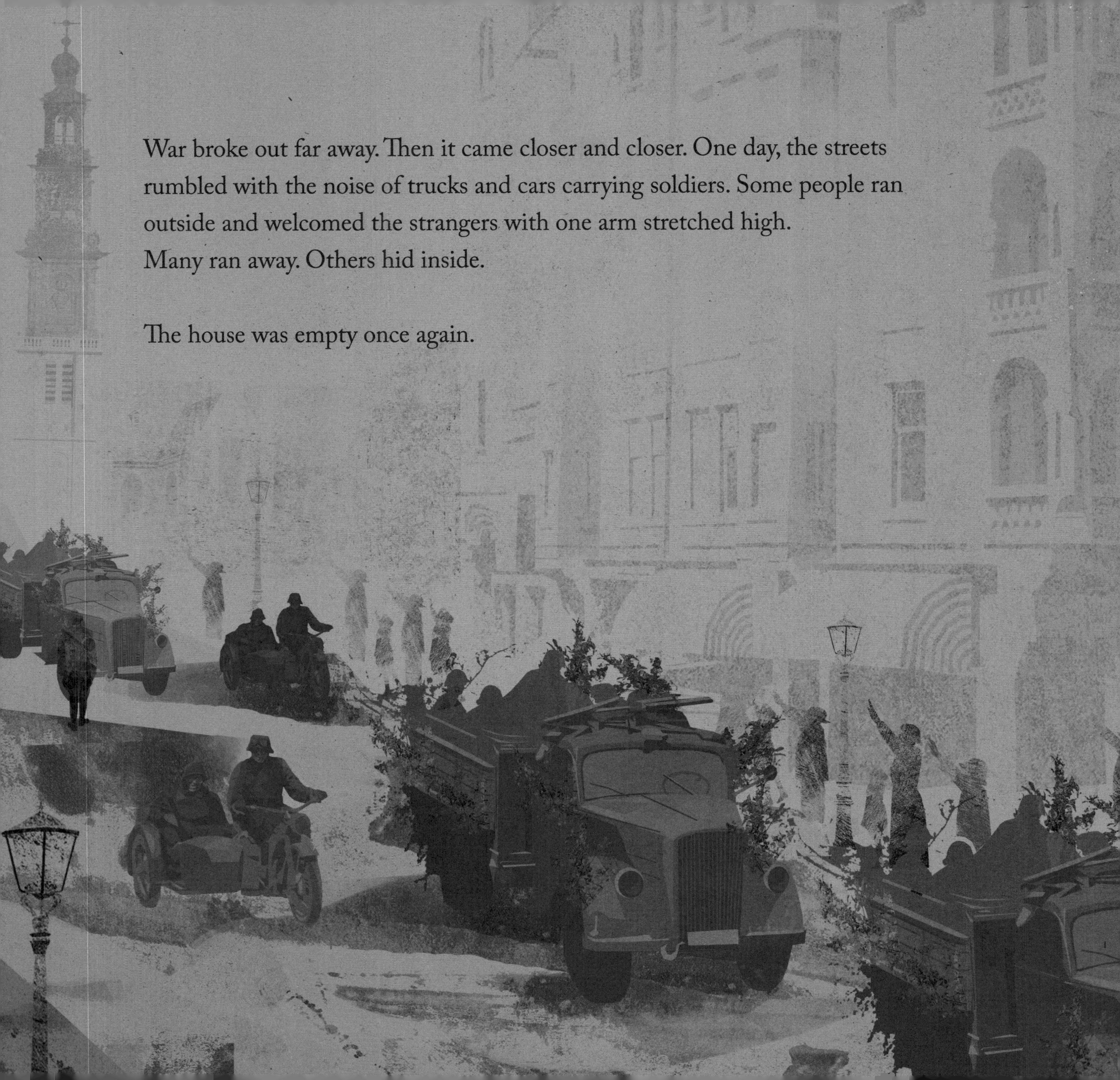

War broke out far away. Then it came closer and closer. One day, the streets rumbled with the noise of trucks and cars carrying soldiers. Some people ran outside and welcomed the strangers with one arm stretched high.
Many ran away. Others hid inside.

The house was empty once again.

1940

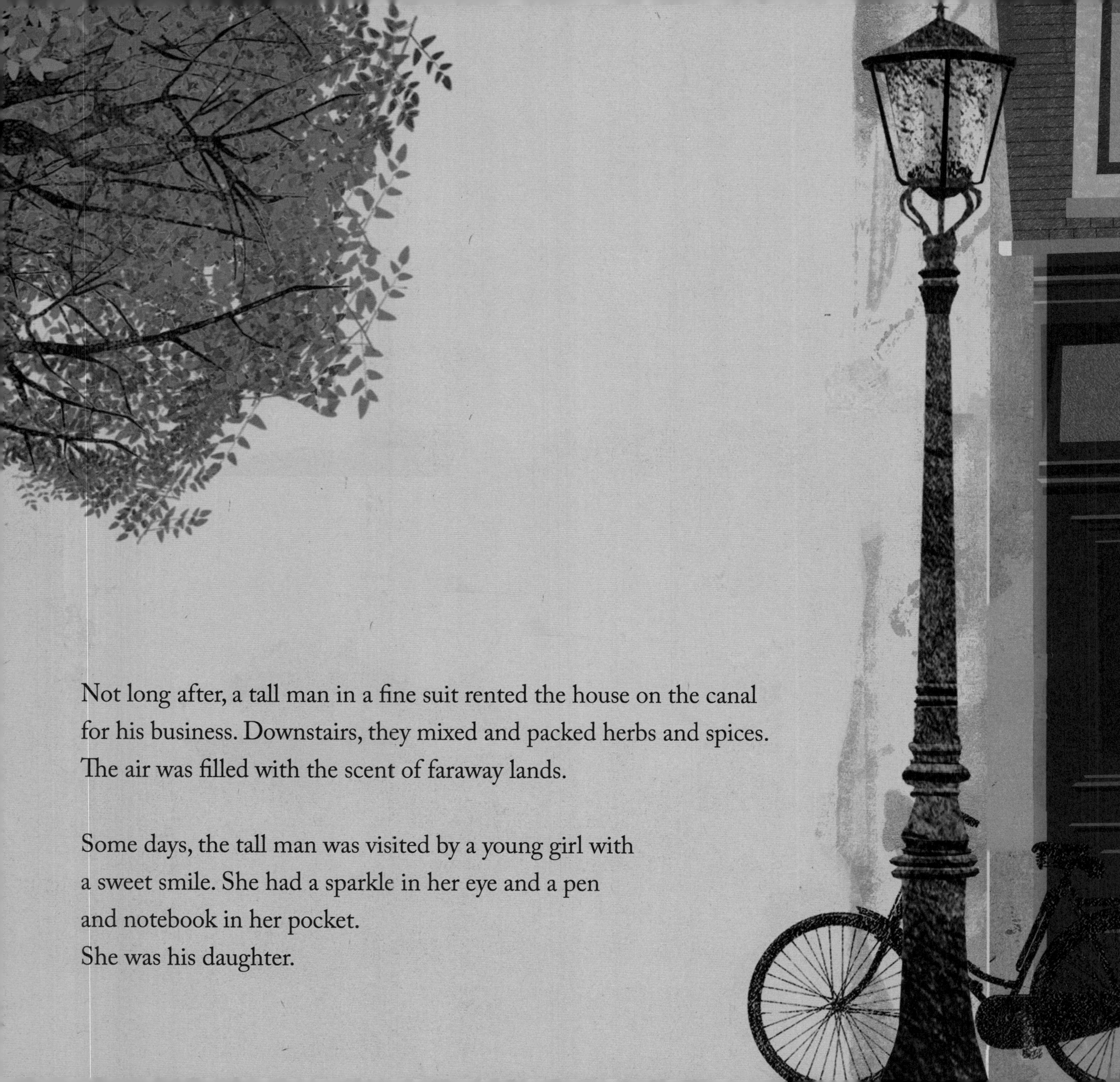

Not long after, a tall man in a fine suit rented the house on the canal for his business. Downstairs, they mixed and packed herbs and spices. The air was filled with the scent of faraway lands.

Some days, the tall man was visited by a young girl with a sweet smile. She had a sparkle in her eye and a pen and notebook in her pocket.
She was his daughter.

1941

Then police and soldiers full of hate came hammering on doors. They were looking for Jews. *BOOM BOOM BOOM.* They shouted for people to come *OUT! OUT! OUT!*

They took them away. They stole people's dreams.

The city was no longer safe for the girl with the sweet smile. The girl with the sweet smile hid in the house with her father and mother and sister and four others. The top floors of the annexe were now a hiding place. They had to be silent, otherwise the police and soldiers would find them.
So still. Not a sound. Each minute was a day. Each day was a year.

They were helped by six friends, who brought them food and things they needed.

All the while, downstairs in the warehouse, the men continued to pack herbs and spices. They were unaware of the hiding place …

… where the young girl wrote in her diary, painting pictures of her days with words.

And after dinner they gathered around a radio and listened to stories from far away.

Shhh… Was that someone coming?
They must be quiet.
Not a peep.

During the night, the girl sneaked upstairs and gazed through the window at the chestnut tree in the garden. She looked up at the stars and the moon and dreamed of a golden future.

And still the world went on outside,
without them.

One hot summer's day, policemen and a soldier came to the house. The men stomped up the secret stairs and found the girl and her family and their friends.

They took them away from the house.

The bells from the church did not ring.

1944

Later, when the police had gone, two kind women picked up the sweet girl's diary and kept it safe.

1944

A cold, cold wind blew through the house. Months went by. Stomachs were empty once again.

Until, one sunny spring morning, soldiers arrived with different uniforms. There was dancing and singing and laughter in the street.

The tall man came back to the house. He was tired and alone. The kind women gave him his daughter's diary, which he read with a crack in his heart and tears in his eyes. And shared with his family.

Then his friends.

And then with the world.

1945

A year passed by, and then another. The house now broke apart. The annexe roof fell down. The windows cracked. Rain poured in. People took the pine floors and the lovely green door.

The house was so sad.

The girl's father worked with the community to clean and repair the house. They fixed the roof and the sturdy pine floors and painted the shiny windows and added a new green front door.

1960

263

Today, people visit the house from far and wide. They learn about the girl with the sweet smile and the diary that she wrote and the house where she lived and her golden dreams of tomorrow.

Once again, the church bells ring –
DONG DONG DONG DONG –
four times every hour.

The Canal

In 1612, construction started in Amsterdam on the Prinsengracht (or Prince's Canal), named after the Prince of Orange (William I). A large church called the Westerkerk was erected next to the Prinsengracht. The canal, church and nearby houses were built during a period of great prosperity in the Netherlands, which is known as the "Golden Age".

The Builder

In 1635, Dirc van Delft purchased a plot of land next to the Prinsengracht. To build the house, he first made a foundation by driving thirteen-metre-long wooden piles into the wet ground. As was typical for this neighbourhood, van Delft added a "rear house" behind the main house, also called an annexe.

The Woman with 12 Children

In 1653, Baefje Bisschop moved into the house with her twelve children. She and her family had suffered persecution because they belonged to a Christian sect called the Remonstrants. In 1663, the neighbourhood was hit with a terrible plague. A few years later, Baefje Bisschop died at the house of old age. Her children moved away. The house was now empty. Temperatures fell below freezing for many months. In 1709, Amsterdam was hit by the "Great Frost"; it was the coldest winter in 500 years.

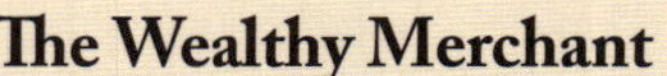

The Wealthy Merchant

In 1740s, Isaac van Vleuten and his wife, Cornelia, moved into the house. They had no children. As with many of his neighbours, van Vleuten made his money partly from slavery. He imported varnish, laudanum, shellac and spices into Amsterdam. Isaac van Vleuten died at the house of old age. His wife Cornelia moved away. The house was used as a horse-barn. It was then abandoned.

Various Businesses

In the 1850s, several businesses were located at the house, including the chemical firm D'Ailly and Dros & Tieleman Brothers, who canned vegetables and meat. Around this time, a chestnut tree was planted in the garden. In 1884, a chimney fire started in the house. Fire trucks were called and put out the flames.

The Ironmonger

In 1901, Alle Pieron moved into the house with his wife and children. His company made metal fireplaces, stoves and beds for missionary hospitals overseas. The family left the house in 1929 and rented it out to various small businesses, including a piano roll maker and a sewing workshop.

On 10 May 1940, Germany invaded the Netherlands. Thousands of Dutch residents waved and cheered as Nazi troops paraded down the streets. This was the start of the German occupation. In 1943, Pieron sold the house to Maurits Alexander Wessels.

Anne Frank

In December 1940, Otto Frank moved his two businesses (Opekta and Pectacon) into the house on the canal. In 1942, the Nazis started rounding up Jews in Amsterdam. Approximately 107,000 Jewish women, men and children were deported from the Netherlands to concentration camps in the east. Of these, only 5,000 survived. To save themselves, the Frank family moved into the top three floors of the annexe. In all, there were eight Jewish people in hiding in the building: Anne Frank; her elder sister, Margot; her father, Otto; her mother, Edith; along with Hermann van Pels; Auguste van Pels; their son, Peter; and a dentist, Fritz Pfeffer. They were helped by six people, of which five worked for Otto Frank's company. While in hiding, Anne kept a diary. On 4 August 1944, Anne Frank and the seven others were discovered and arrested by the Dutch police, led by a German officer, and deported to concentration camps. Otto Frank was the only one to survive the camps. Anne's diary was discovered in the annexe by Miep Gies and Bep Voskuijl, who worked in Otto's business. Miep gave it to Otto when he returned to Amsterdam in June 1945. It was first published in 1947.

The Anne Frank House

After the war, the house was purchased by NV Berghaus, a business who wanted to demolish the building and build a large warehouse. Otto Frank and others managed to convince NV Berghaus to donate the building to the city instead. In 1960, after an extensive renovation programme, the house was opened to the public. Today, the Anne Frank House is visited by more than a million people a year. It is a museum and a centre for education.

Thomas Harding, born in 1968, is a multi-award-winning bestselling author whose books have been translated into over nineteen languages. As a journalist, he has written for *The Guardian, The Washington Post* and other newspapers and works as a radio and television presenter. He is chairman of Alexander Haus e.V. and lives with his family in the UK.

Britta Teckentrup, born in 1969, is an award-winning artist and author. She studied at St Martin's College and the Royal College of Art in London and has written and illustrated over a hundred children's books, which have been translated into more than 25 languages. She lives with her family in Berlin.

First published 2023 as *Das alte Haus an der Gracht*

Published in the UK 2025 by Walker Studio
an imprint of Walker Books Ltd, 87 Vauxhall Walk, London SE11 5HJ

Text: Thomas Harding
Illustrations: Britta Teckentrup
Printed in China

ISBN 978-1-5295-2032-3

With gratitude to the Anne Frank Stichting, Amsterdam,
for their support: annefrank.org/de/

WALKER STUDIO
AN IMPRINT OF WALKER BOOKS

www.walkerstudio.com